KUN-MAN-GUR

◎

THE RAINBOW SERPENT

BY

JAMES COWAN

ILLUSTRATIONS BY

BRONWYN BANCROFT

BAREFOOT BOOKS

BOSTON & BATH

BAREFOOT BOOKS, INC.

Horticultural Hall

300 Massachusetts Avenue

Boston, Massachusetts 02115

Text © 1994 by James Cowan

Illustrations © 1994 by Bronwyn Bancroft

First published in Great Britain in 1994 by Barefoot Books Ltd

First published in the United States of America in 1994 by Barefoot Books, Inc.

Printed in Belgium by Proost International Book Production

ISBN 1 56957 906 7

Library of Congress Cataloging-in-Publication-Data

Cowan, James,1942

Kun-man-gur the Rainbow Serpent/by James Cowan; illustrations by Bronwyn Bancroft.

p. cm.

"First Published in Great Britain 1994 by Barefoot Books" − T.p.verso.

Summary: In this telling of an Aboriginal creation myth, the Rainbow Serpent, Kun-man-gur, finds home and food for the
flying foxes after he punishes a bat for saying that they smelled bad. Includes a foreword explaining the background and
importance of the myth.

ISBN 1 56957 906 7 (acid-free paper)

[1. Creation. 2. Australian aboriginies − legends.] I. Bancroft, Bronwyn, ill. II. Title: Kun-man-gur the Rainbow Serpent.

PZ8.1.C816KU 1994

398.21'089'9915-dc20

93-32319

CIP-AC

KUN-MAN-GUR

◉

THE RAINBOW SERPENT

FOREWORD

The Rainbow Serpent is the principal culture hero among the Aborigines of north Australia. The Serpent is both male and female, thus embodying certain aspects of the mother-womb and father-phallus. As the regenerative source of life, the Rainbow Serpent is responsible for the renewal of all creatures, great and small. It lives in waterholes, and is also responsible for the creation of rivers at the time of the Dreaming.

The Aborigines revere this spirit-being above all others. Cave walls throughout the north are daubed with its image, and major ritual cycles embodying the feminine aspect of the Great Snake are performed each year in its honor, these being made up of hundreds of songs, many dances, and a host of stories about the serpent. Participating in these rites is, for boys, an important step on the way to fully initiated adulthood. Broadly speaking, the Great Snake is regarded as female among the tribes of north Australia. In the desert regions, and in the Kimberley of north-west Australia, the Rainbow Serpent takes on a more specifically male aspect, though in all cases gender characteristics remain ambivalent.

Its sexual duality means that in many regions of the country the Rainbow Serpent is also known as the Great Mother or Kunapipi. As Kunapipi, she is believed to have created men and women, determined their kin groups (totemic), and given them the sacred law. Her incarnation is the incarnation of the Eternal Feminine which unfolds in the history of humanity as the history of every individual woman.

The Rainbow Serpent is nearly always associated with water. So ancient is its lineage that it predates the many-breasted Diana of Ephesus, the goddess Nut in Egyptian cosmology, and the Indian goddess Kali. In the Great Snake male and female are united: her avid womb attracts the male and engulfs the phallus, which then resides as a potentiality within herself.

The Rainbow Serpent's invisible presence is often associated with the sound of the bullroarer (a length of wood attached to a cord and whirled around the head), which is said to send forth "flashes of lightning like the tongue of a snake." In one depiction of the Rainbow Serpent myth, Djangawul, who like Kun-man-gur is the masculine aspect of the Great Snake, engages in incestuous activity with two of his sisters at the time of the Dreaming. He regularly places his hand in their wombs in order to draw forth the ancestors of the Aborigines, so that they may populate the land.

As a culture hero, the Rainbow Serpent acts as a bridge to the realm of the Dreaming itself. The Dreaming is a metaphysical condition wherein the world was created. Aborigines acknowledge that, prior to this moment, the world was "without form" – was in fact a flat, featureless plain. Culture heroes like the Rainbow Serpent emerged from the earth to begin the process of world-creation, and so created Australia.

The Dreaming, however, is not an event that occurs "in time." According to the Aborigines, the Dreaming is ever-present – men and women participate in it each time they enact the sacred rituals. *Lalan* or *Alcheringa*, the Aboriginal words for the Dreaming, both mean the "time of ancestors." Thus the Dreaming describes that pristine moment when humankind enters into a stage of (self)-consciousness, while preserving a sense of the ever-renewing nature of life itself.

All of the many Aboriginal myths recording the world-creation by the culture heroes celebrate the events of the Dreaming. The entire continent of Australia is one vast "storyline," being a series of narratives that detail the progress of the Rainbow Serpent across the earth. It is possible to follow one of these storylines and so recreate the Dreaming for oneself – provided, of course, that one is in the company of an Aboriginal elder who can sing the songs along the Dreaming track.

At another level, of course, Kun-man-gur is a genuine avatar. Not only has he helped to create all that appears in the world, as a figure from outside the world, but he is also responsible for the creation of Aboriginal value systems. Beneath the surface of the Great Snake's often paradoxical activity we see the generation of tribal ethics and values. In this sense he is avataric.

Children are introduced to the reality of the Rainbow Serpent at an early age. More often than not they are taught its fearful aspects so that when they attain the age of puberty, they know their encounter with the Great Snake during initiation ceremonies will have a powerful effect on them. In a sense, the Great Snake represents the invisible aspect of deity made manifest.

In this story of Kun-man-gur we see the Rainbow Serpent as world-creator extend his efforts to selecting the different kinds of food eaten by flying foxes, as well as separating individual animal species – in this case bats and flying foxes. (Aborigines regard bats and flying foxes as being different from one another.) We are also introduced to the regenerative power of the Great Snake. It is both womb, depicted by a fishing net, and phallus, depicted by a bamboo rod, to the people nurtured in its watery cavern.

It must also be emphasized that, while the myth speaks of animals, we are in fact dealing with anthropomorphic figures. The bats and flying foxes are not only animals but also the antecedents of the Aborigines, since the Aborigines, through their totemic affiliations, believe themselves to be derived from individual animals at the time of the Dreaming.

The Kun-man-gur myth was first related to Roland Robinson (*Aboriginal Myths and Legends*, Sun Books, 1968) by Kianoo Tjeemairee of the Murrinpatha Tribe, Port Keats, Northern Territory, Australia. We are grateful to the Murrinpatha people for giving us permission to interpret their myth.

James Cowan

KUN-MAN-GUR
THE RAINBOW SERPENT

One day a bat named Kunbul was sitting alone by his fire in the bush. Two flying foxes saw his smoke and decided to join him. Their names were Warlet and Ninji.

When Warlet and Ninji sat down, Kunbul thought they smelled bad. He wrinkled his nose.

"Aah chew!" Kunbul sneezed. "You fellas don't smell right to me."

Warlet and Ninji looked at one another.

"What's wrong with us?" Warlet asked.

"You smell different – isn't that enough?" Kunbul answered.

Warlet and Ninji were shocked by Kunbul's bad manners. They thought everyone smelled the same, you see. They didn't like being told that they were different. So they decided to tell their father, old Kun-man-gur the Rainbow Serpent, what Kunbul the bat had said to them.

They found him sleeping on the bank of the river.

"Kunbul said we smelled bad," cried Warlet.

"I think maybe we should teach Kunbul a lesson," added Ninji.

Old Kun-man-gur the Rainbow Serpent thought about what his sons had told him concerning Kunbul. He too thought maybe Kunbul should be taught a lesson. After all, people were very much the same, whatever their shape or size. It did not matter whether they chose to call themselves flying foxes or bats.

"All right," he said. "Call all your flying-fox friends together, and give Kunbul the bat a good beating."

Meanwhile a friend of Kunbul, the toad-fish Ngar-in-gara, sat down near Kunbul's fire. He puffed up his gills and growled at Kunbul.

"Why did you tell Warlet and Ninji they smell so bad?" he demanded.

"Because they do," Kunbul shot back angrily.

"You're in big trouble," Ngar-in-gara said. "I hear the flying-fox boys are on their way over here to give you a beating."

"I'm too good for them," replied Kunbul, flapping his dark wings. "After all, I can see at night with my ears. They won't be able to catch me. They're only flying foxes," he added.

"Well, here's your chance to prove yourself," Ngar-in-gara replied. "I see Warlet and Ninji with all the flying foxes flying toward us right now."

Sure enough, dozens of flying foxes were approaching in two lines behind Warlet and Ninji. Each flying fox was painted in red or white ochre. When they saw Kunbul the bat and Ngar-in-gara the toad-fish, they prepared for battle.

"We'll see who smells bad when this is all over," Warlet called out.

"Maybe you will be the one who smells worse than us," said Ninji as he threw the first spear at Kunbul.

Spears rained down on Kunbul from all directions. He jumped this way and that to escape them. Ngar-in-gara also jumped about, and not one spear hit him either.

"Hah! You can't spear us!" cried Kunbul.

"We're too fast for you!" Ngar-in-gara laughed.

Meanwhile old Kun-man-gur the Rainbow Serpent climbed out of his waterhole and slithered up the riverbank to watch the battle. He saw Kunbul and the toad-fish jumping this way and that, like butterflies. He watched Warlet and Ninji and their friends throwing spear after spear. Soon the ground looked like a forest of poles.

Kun-man-gur felt sorry for the flying foxes. So he secretly caused one of the spears to soar through the air and hit Kunbul. The spear wounded Kunbul in the leg, so that he fell to the ground.

"Ouch!" Kunbul cried out in pain.

"Hey, let me help you," the toad-fish Ngar-in-gara called as he ran to help his friend.

Ngar-in-gara pulled the spear out of Kunbul, and then placed the wounded bat over his shoulders.

"Let's get out of here," he whispered as he carried Kunbul into the safety of the bush, away from the forest of spears.

"Who smells bad now!" Warlet teased Kunbul.

Meanwhile all the flying foxes gathered round old Kun-man-gur the Rainbow Serpent to thank him for his help. Kun-man-gur flashed his forked tongue and smiled.

"What will we do now, old man?" Warlet asked Kun-man-gur.

"This country belongs to us, now that Kunbul and his friend have run away," said Ninji.

But old Kun-man-gur shook his towering head.

"You belong in the mangrove swamps, not here on dry land," he told them. "Anyway," he added, "you can't live where there are no flowers to eat."

"But I want to stay," Warlet argued.

"You must obey me," the Rainbow Serpent hissed. "Come down to the bottom of the river where I live."

When they had reached the riverbank, old Kun-mar-gur cut down a piece of hollow bamboo. This he filled with all the flying foxes, including Warlet and Ninji. He pushed them in so tightly that he could barely plug the hole. What flying foxes were left over he put into his fishing net. Then he dragged the piece of bamboo and his fishing net down to the bottom of the river.

"All day you can stay down here with me," Kun-man-gur bubbled. "When the flowers come out, I will free you so that you can eat them."

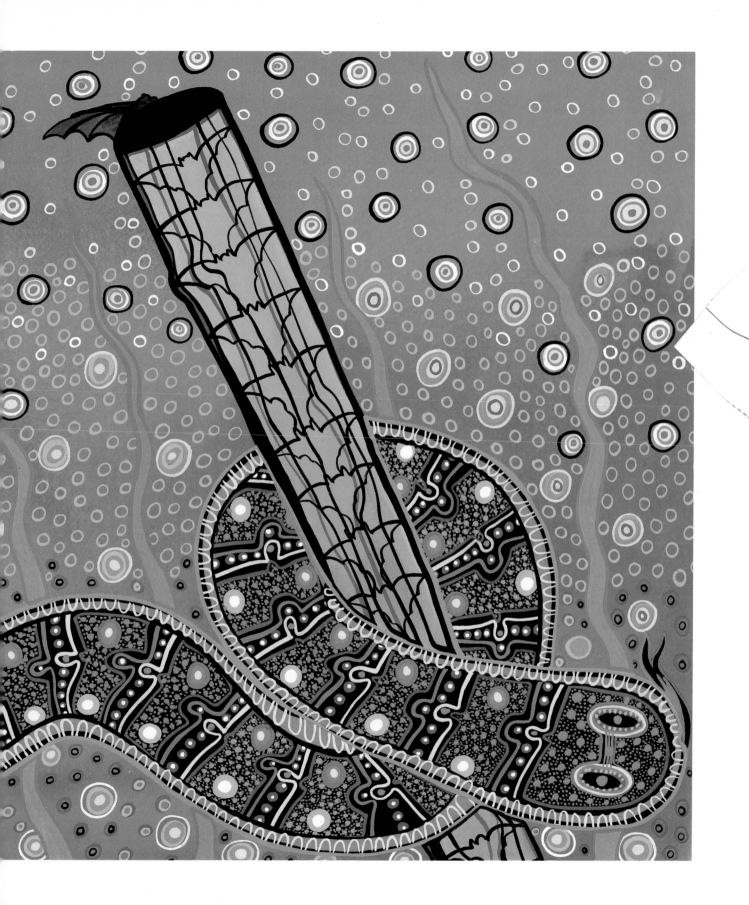

So each day old Kun-man-gur would rise up out of the water to his full height. He would look about to see whether the trees were covered in flowers. As he did so, he would call out the name of each tree.

"Hey you, gum tree! Where are your red flowers?"

And Kunmurrin the gum tree blossomed red with flowers.

"Hey you, Pirroo! Where are your white flowers?"

And Pirroo, another gum tree, blossomed white with flowers.

"Hey you, paper-bark tree, where are your flowers?"

And Werr the paper-bark tree blossomed even whiter with flowers.

Now Kun-man-gur opened up the length of bamboo filled with his flying-fox children, and blew them into the air.

"Where's my food?" cried Warlet as he fluttered about.

"You may eat the red flowers of Kunmurrin," the Rainbow Serpent answered.

"Where is my food?" Ninji echoed.

"You may eat the white flowers of Pirroo and Werr," the Rainbow Serpent answered. "They are your food."

And old Kun-man-gur the Rainbow Serpent again rose up out of the water, calling the names of the different trees once again. As he did so, more trees rose from the ground as if by magic.

"Oh, Binni the bloodwood, how tasty you are!" he cried.

"Oh, Kowan the white-gum tree, your food is so sweet!" he called.

"Oh, Manak the iron-wood tree, your food is best when your flowers have dropped."

Then Kun-man-gur set loose more flying foxes from his fishing net so that they, too, flew up into the trees to eat. The sky was dark with flying foxes, all chasing after different-colored tree blossoms.

"You're free to fly wherever you please," the Rainbow Serpent told his children. "You may feed all night. But at dawn you must always return to me. You promise?"

"Don't worry," Warlet and Ninji promised. "We'll come back before the sun rises."

The flying foxes were true to their word. At dawn each morning they flew back to where Kun-man-gur lay on the riverbank. The Rainbow Serpent squeezed them into the hollow bamboo and into his fishing net as he had done before. Then he dragged them down to the bottom of the river to sleep. But on one occasion a young flying fox refused to join his friends. His name was Yoorinja. He didn't like flowers, it seemed. He preferred a different kind of food.

"All right," Kun-man-gur said to tiny Yoorinja. "Next time we'll follow you up river on the tide. Maybe you can take us to where you have found new food."

So little Yoorinja guided the flying foxes to a new and tastier feeding place. Soon all the flying foxes were hanging upside down in the trees, licking their lips. They too had discovered what little Yoorinja enjoyed most – honey, of course!

This is how Kun-man-gur the Rainbow Serpent helped his children the flying foxes when the world was new. He chased away silly Kunbul the bat and the toad-fish Ngar-in-gara because they were so rude to the flying foxes. And he showed Warlet and Ninji and their friends the right flowers to eat each night. He taught them to like honey, too.

To this day Kun-man-gur the Rainbow Serpent puts the hollow bamboo to his mouth and blows flying foxes all over the earth. He turns them loose from his fishing net, too. Whenever he does this, he sprays water high into the air, so that it arcs over his head to form a rainbow. This is how old Kun-man-gur gets his name.

For Kun-man-gur is the rainbow in the sky.